SANTA *KNOWS*. . .

A man with a bushy white beard and a red coat was driving the car next to them. He had on a red hat with a white pom-pom.

"It sure looks like him," said Gramps.

"He's here!" Posey shouted. She bounced up and down. "He's really here! Just like the song says!"

The song.

Posey stopped bouncing.

Santa knew when they were bad or good. That must mean he knew what Posey did.

What if he didn't come to her house on Christmas?

OTHER BOOKS YOU MAY ENJOY

PRINCESS POSEY

and the

CHRISTMAS MAGIC

Stephanie Greene

ILLUSTRATED BY

Stephanie Roth Sisson

PUFFIN BOOKS

An Imprint of Penguin Group (USA)

PUFFIN BOOKS
Published by the Penguin Group
Penguin Group (USA) LLC
375 Hudson Street
New York, New York 10014

USA * Canada * UK * Ireland * Australia
New Zealand * India * South Africa * China

penguin.com
A Penguin Random House Company

Published simultaneously in the United States of America by G. P. Putnam's Sons and Puffin Books,
divisions of Penguin Young Readers Group, 2013

THE LIBRARY OF CONGRESS HAS CATALOGED THE G. P. PUTNAM'S SONS EDITION AS FOLLOWS:
Greene, Stephanie.
Princess Posey and the Christmas magic / Stephanie Greene ;
illustrated by Stephanie Roth Sisson.
pages cm
Summary: Posey and her family and friends prepare for the holidays.
ISBN 978-0-399-16363-0 (hardcover)
[1. Christmas—Fiction.] I. Sisson, Stephanie Roth, illustrator. II. Title.
PZ7.G8434Pm 2013
[Fic]—dc23
2012046089

Puffin Books ISBN 978-0-14-242734-7

Decorative graphics by Marikka Tamura. Design by Marikka Tamura.

Printed in the United States of America

3 5 7 9 10 8 6 4 2

For Donna and Barbara,
magic lifelong friends.
—S.G.

To Miss Lucy Shrubb,
my sparkly artist friend.
—S.R.S.

CONTENTS

CHAPTER ONE

SANTA CLAUS IS COMING TO TOWN

It was almost Christmas. In Miss Lee's class, they were learning about holidays around the world.

"People in different countries celebrate for different reasons," Miss Lee said.

"They celebrate Christmas," Luca shouted.

"Some of them do, Luca. But people celebrate other holidays as well," said Miss Lee. "Does anyone know what some of them are called?"

Feliz Navidad!

Kwanzaa!

"Hanukkah," said Ava.

"Kwanzaa," said Robert.

"Chinese New Year," said Grace.

"Feliz Navidad!" Freddy shouted.

"Freddy said 'Happy Christmas' in Spanish." Miss Lee smiled. "You're all right."

They ran outside when it was time for recess. Posey sat on the swings with Ava, Nikki, and Grace.

"Let's sing the song about Santa Claus coming to town," said Posey.

It was Posey's favorite song. It was so exciting to think about Santa flying over her town. His sleigh would be full of presents. He would land on Posey's own roof.

"He sees you when you're sleeping. He knows when you're awake," they sang as they pumped.

"He knows if you've been bad or good, so be good for goodness' sake!"

They sang the last part loud.

"Now let's sing one on the slide!" Grace shouted.

They jumped off the swings and ran to the slide.

"This year, I'm going to stay awake so I hear the reindeer bells," Posey said.

"I heard them last year," said Nikki.

"You're so lucky," said Posey.

"We don't have a
roof in our apartment,"
Ava said. "We only have
a ceiling."

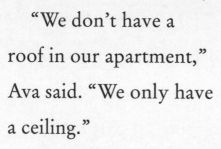

"Santa can go anywhere,"
said Grace.

The boys were pretending
to be superheroes. They swung on
the monkey bars and yelled. They
were so noisy.

"Oh, for goodness' sake!" Posey
shouted. "Be quiet!"

"For goodness' sake!" her
friends shouted.

"If I had a magic wand, I could
make them disappear," said Posey.

"You could turn them into
frogs," Grace said.

"You could turn them into teeny, tiny ants," said Nikki.

The girls giggled.

"I could do anything, if it was real," said Posey.

It would be so much fun if Santa brought her a real magic wand for Christmas.

A LETTER TO SANTA

On the weekend, Posey and her mom and Danny and Gramps shopped for their Christmas tree.

"How about this one?" Gramps asked.

"Too skinny," said Posey.

"You said the two before this were too fat." Gramps held out another tree. "This one any good?"

Posey shook her head.

"Posey has strong opinions about her Christmas tree," her mom said. She was holding Danny.

"You're telling me," said Gramps. He pulled out another tree. "What do you think about this one, Miss Christmas Tree Expert?"

Posey looked at it from all sides.

It was cheerful and round. Like a friendly person.

"That's the one," she said.

"Danny?" said Gramps. "Let's hear your vote."

"Twee!" Danny cried.

"I guess this one's the winner," said Gramps.

Gramps tied the tree on top of the car. When they got home, he leaned it against the garage.

"I have to cut a piece off the bottom," he said. "I will bring it in when I'm finished."

"We'll make hot chocolate while we wait," Posey's mom said. "Posey can work on her letter to Santa."

"I wrote it already," said Posey. "I told him I want a magic wand."

"What about the wand you made?" her mom asked.

"I want a real one," Posey said.

"Seems to me if you want magic to happen, you have to make it happen yourself," said Gramps.

Gramps and her mom didn't understand. But Posey knew Santa would.

She had covered the bottom of her letter with purple and pink X's and O's.

Dear Santa,

→ Rudolf

Please bring me

✻ a pet that's alive
✻ books
✻ something sparkly to wear
✻ glow-in-the-dark stars
✻ bubble bath
✻ a small house for Poinky

✩ a magic wand that really works, this is my <u>favorite</u> present. I want it more than anything.

X X O O X O X O X O Posey

When Santa saw it, he would know how much Posey wanted a magic wand that really worked.

CHAPTER THREE

THE MOST BEAUTIFUL TREE IN THE WORLD

Mrs. Romero came to see the tree when it got dark.

Gramps turned off the lights in the living room. Posey tied a towel over Mrs. Romero's eyes. She led her to the doorway.

Her mom and Danny were waiting for them.

"Ready?" said Gramps.

"Ready!" Posey shouted.

The tree burst into light. It lit up the room like a giant, sparkling candle. The lights were red and green and yellow and blue.

"That's the most beautiful tree I've seen in my whole life," said Mrs. Romero.

"In my whole life, too," said Posey.

Danny walked over and reached out to grab a shiny ornament.

"No, Danny," his mom said. She gently pulled his hand back. "Don't touch."

Mrs. Romero stayed for dinner. They had so much fun.

Gramps had fixed Mrs. Romero's front door. Now they were friends.

Mrs. Romero's name was Norma. Gramps teased her by calling her "Normal" all through dinner.

"Wait a minute," Gramps said. "Are you normal or Norma?"

Mrs. Romero laughed every time.

After dinner, Posey carried a plate of brownies into the living room. She put them on the table in front of the couch. She turned around. Danny was next to the tree.

"Don't touch, Danny," Posey said in her big-sister voice.

Danny didn't listen. He grabbed a shiny ornament.

"No, Danny!" Posey said.

She rushed over and pushed
Danny back. He landed on his
bottom. The ornament
broke.

Danny held
up his hand and roared.

Posey saw a small dot of red on
his finger. She had hurt her baby
brother!

"What happened?" Posey's mom called from the kitchen.

Posey was so afraid. She didn't know what to do. It was an accident.

"Danny fell," Posey told her mom when she came into the room.

"Oh, dear. Let me see." Her mom picked up Danny and looked at his hand.

"Is there blood?" said Posey.

"Only a tiny bit." Her mom kissed the tip of Danny's finger one, two, three times. "All gone," she said.

"He grabbed it," Posey said. Her eyes were stinging. "I told him no, but he didn't listen."

"He scared himself more than anything," her mom said. "Poor little guy. Let's go get you into your pajamas."

Posey had an empty hole inside when her mom left. She wished her mom had kissed her, too.

She wished she had told her mom what really happened.

Now it was too late.

CHAPTER FOUR

SANTA'S HERE!

Gramps picked up Posey after school the next day.

"We have to stop and get butter," Gramps said. "Mrs. Romero

is going to show us how to make her Christmas cookies."

"You like Mrs. Romero, don't you, Gramps?" said Posey.

"Yes, I do," he said.

"Do you like her a lot?"

"I like her just fine, little matchmaker," said Gramps. "What did you learn at school today?"

Posey started to tell him. Then she stopped. Her eyes got huge.

"Gramps!" she shouted. "It's him! Look! It's Santa Claus!"

A man with a bushy white beard and a red coat was driving the car next to them. He had on a red hat with a white pom-pom.

"It sure looks like him," said Gramps.

"He's here!" Posey shouted.
She bounced up and down.
"He's here! The real Santa Claus!
Just like the song says!"

Oh, no. The song. He knows if
you've been bad or good.

Posey stopped bouncing. What if Santa saw what Posey did to Danny?

He would know she didn't tell her mom. He would think Posey was bad.

"We can leave him some of Mrs. Romero's cookies," Gramps said. "He looks like a three-cookie man to me."

Posey couldn't tell Gramps that Santa might not come to her house. He would be too disappointed.

So she didn't say a word.

CHAPTER FIVE

AN ANGEL
IN HEAVEN

Gramps pulled into the driveway.

"You got awfully quiet all of a sudden," Gramps said. "Do you have one of your excitement stomachaches again?"

"A little bit," said Posey.

"Do you want to go inside?" Gramps asked. "Or can you go next door and tell Mrs. Romero we have all of her ingredients?"

"I'll go tell her."

Posey went to Mrs. Romero's back door and knocked.

"Come in!" Mrs. Romero called.

"It's me," said Posey. Hero ran up to her when she opened the door.

"I'm in the living room," Mrs. Romero said.

"Gramps said to tell you that we got butter," Posey told her.

Mrs. Romero looked up from a picture she was holding. "Wonderful."

She looked back at the picture. "Have I ever shown you this?"

Posey stood next to her. It was a photograph of a little girl with long brown hair. She had on a blue bathing suit.

"Who is it?" Posey asked.

"My little girl, Barbara," said Mrs. Romero.

"She was about your age in this picture."

"Where is she now?" said Posey.

"She's in heaven."

"You mean she died?" said Posey.

"Yes."

"Why?"

"It was a long time ago," Mrs. Romero said. "She had a sickness the doctors couldn't fix."

"Are you still sad?"

"Only sometimes," Mrs. Romero said. "Most of the time, it makes me very happy to think about her. She's my angel in heaven."

"I bet Barbara liked Christmas," Posey said.

"Did she ever!" Mrs. Romero

laughed. "She tried so hard to stay awake on Christmas Eve."

"That's like me," said Posey.

Mrs. Romero put the picture on the shelf.

"I will tell you more about her someday," Mrs. Romero said. "But we had better get going if we're going to make those cookies."

❁ ❁ ❁

"Mom," Posey said when she got into bed. "Did you know Mrs. Romero had a little girl who died?"

"Yes," her mom said.

"Her name was Barbara."

"I know."

"Mrs. Romero's still sad," said
Posey.

"She will probably always be a little sad," her mom said. She tucked Posey in tight. "But I know it makes her very happy to have you next door."

"I love Mrs. Romero," Posey said.

"She loves you, too," said her mom.

When her mom left, Posey went and got her pink tutu. She took  it under the covers with her. She held it tight.

Things were so mixed up.

Posey was happy it was Christmas. But she was sad about Mrs. Romero and not telling her mom what really happened.

Before, she wanted a magic wand that really worked. Now she had to have one. She could use it to make everything better.

If Santa didn't come to her house, she wouldn't get one.

Posey's worries made a little secret knot in her stomach.

CHAPTER
SIX

GRAMPS
AND HIS
TWO LEFT FEET

On Saturday, Posey helped Gramps hang a wreath on the front door. Its ribbon was crooked.

"Fish sticks!" said Gramps. That was what Gramps always said when he was annoyed.

He moved the wreath. The ribbon was still crooked. "This stubborn thing won't cooperate," Gramps said.

Posey went to find her mom when they got inside.

"I think there's something wrong with Gramps," she said.

"What do you mean?" said her mom.

"He's acting grouchy," Posey whispered.

Her mom laughed. "That's because he and Mrs. Romero are going on a date," she whispered back.

"A date?" Posey shouted. "Gramps!" She ran into the living room. "You and Mrs. Romero have a date?"

"I knew your mom couldn't keep a secret," Gramps grumbled.

"But you like Mrs. Romero," said Posey.

"Not when she wants me to take her dancing."

"Dancing is fun," said Posey.

"Not for me it isn't," Gramps said. "I have two left feet."

Posey laughed. "No one has two left feet."

"You want to bet?" said Gramps.

"I can teach you!" Posey shouted. "I'll be right back."

Posey ran up to her room. She put on her pink tutu and her veil.

She was Princess Posey.

Princess Posey could go any-where and do anything. All by herself.

Even teach her grouchy gramps how to dance.

Posey ran back downstairs.

"Watch," she told Gramps. "This is all you have to do."

Posey leaped and twirled. She jumped and kicked. She sang as loudly as she could. Dancing made her so happy.

"See?" Posey said when her dance was over. "It's easy."

"You're as pretty as a ballerina in a music box," Gramps said. "But I think Mrs. Romero has a different kind of dancing in mind."

"You mean the kind where the boy and girl hold each other," said Posey.

"You got it." Gramps stood up. He held open his arms. "I guess we might as well give it a try. Maybe you can work a miracle."

Posey stood on the top of Gramps's shoes. He put his arm around her and started to hum.

At first they went slowly.

Then they went faster

and faster
and faster.

"That was fun!" Posey said when they stopped.

"I didn't step on your feet once," Gramps said proudly.

"That's because my feet were on top of yours," said Posey.

"I guess I'll have to ask Mrs. Romero to step up there, too," said Gramps.

AN IMPORTANT PICTURE

It was the last day of school before Christmas vacation.

Posey carried the cookies she had made with Mrs. Romero into her classroom. They were for Miss Lee's party. Everyone had brought something to eat.

After the party, they were all too excited to work. Miss Lee's room got louder and louder.

"You know what?" Miss Lee said. "I think we need a little quiet reading time."

She pressed a button on her music player. "I want you to pretend you're little mice and find a cozy spot to read."

Soft music started to play.

"Shhh." Miss Lee held her finger to her lips. "The cat might be near. Quiet as mice."

Everyone started to tiptoe. Children curled up under their desks and in the corners of the room. Some sat on cushions in the reading corner.

Posey went up to Miss Lee's desk. "Can I draw instead of read?" she asked.

"I don't know how you have any ideas left after all of the drawings you've done," Miss Lee said.

"I still do," said Posey.

"Is it important?" Miss Lee asked.

Posey nodded.

"Okay, then." Miss Lee smiled.
"Do it quietly."

Posey got a piece of paper and
some crayons.

Her drawing was very
important.

AN ANGEL
HERE ON EARTH

Mrs. Romero
opened her
kitchen door when
Posey knocked.

"I made this for you," Posey said. She held out her present.

"For me? How exciting," said Mrs. Romero. "Come in. Get out of the cold."

Posey went into the warm kitchen. It smelled of spaghetti.

Mrs. Romero sat down at the table. "Can I open it now, or do I have to wait for Christmas?" she asked.

"You can open it now," Posey said.

"Oh, goody." Mrs. Romero laughed. "I know I should act

more grown up. But I love presents."

When Mrs. Romero saw Posey's drawing, her face got very still.

"It's Barbara," Posey said. "Do you like it?"

"I love it," Mrs. Romero said. "It's the most wonderful present anyone has ever given me."

Posey leaned against her.

"I glued on a ribbon for her hair," said Posey. "There wasn't brown, so I used yellow."

"How did you make her wings so sparkly?" Mrs. Romero asked.

"I used glitter glue," Posey said.

"I used it for her halo, too."

Mrs. Romero slanted the drawing this way and that. Barbara's wings and halo sparkled.

"I can't get over it," said Mrs. Romero. "It's as if you waved a magic wand and lifted up my heart."

"You can put it next to the picture of Barbara," said Posey. "Then you will have two angels."

"I will have three." Mrs. Romero pulled Posey close. "You're my real, live angel here on earth."

THE SECRET KNOT
COMES LOOSE

It was Christmas Eve morning. Gramps was coming to take them to the Christmas parade.

Posey was on her bed in her pajamas. Her stuffed animals were lined up in front of her.

Posey told them about her secret knot. They were very kind. They told Posey she was just a little girl. They said everything would be all right.

It made Posey feel a little better. Now she had to tell her mom to feel all the way better.

She got out of bed and put on her pink tutu.

Princess Posey could do anything.

Even something hard.

Her mom was making pancakes. Posey stopped in the kitchen door.

"Mom?" said Posey.

Her mom turned around. "Why such a long face on Christmas Eve day?" she asked.

"I have to tell you something bad."

"Posey, what is it?" Her mom put down her spoon.

"Santa Claus might not come to our house," said Posey. Everything got blurry.

Gramps had come in from outside.

"Might not come?" he said. "Of course he will."

Posey's mom sat down and pulled Posey onto her lap. "What's this all about?" she said in a gentle voice.

The secret knot came loose. All of Posey's worries flooded out.

"I need a real magic wand," Posey cried. "But Santa knows I told a lie."

"Sweetie, it was my fault," said her mom. "I never should have put a breakable ornament where Danny could reach it."

"You're the best little girl in the world," Gramps said. "Who drew the picture that made Mrs. Romero so happy?"

"Me." Posey sniffed.

"Who made a man with two left feet brave enough to dance on his date?"

"Me."

"Did you need a magic wand to do those things?" Gramps shook his head. "No. You did them yourself."

"Gramps is right." Posey's mom hugged her tight. She kissed Posey's wet face. "You never have to be afraid to tell me when something happens, okay?"

"Okay."

"Feel better now?" her mom said.

Posey nodded. The secret knot was gone.

Danny yelled and banged his cup on his high chair.

Posey's mom laughed. "I think Danny feels left out," she said.

"I'm with you, Danny. Let's get this show on the road," said Gramps. He lifted Danny out of his high chair and put him on his shoulders.

Danny grabbed Gramps's hair.

"Are we going to this parade or
not?" Gramps said.

"We're going!" Posey cried.

"Like that?" her
mom asked.

Posey looked down. She had on her pajamas under her tutu.

"For goodness' sake!" Posey shouted. "I'll be right back!"

❀ ❀ ❀

That night, Posey tried to keep her eyes open so she could hear the reindeer. She tried and she tried.

But her eyes got heavy. They slowly drifted shut.

The next thing she knew, it was Christmas.

A WORLD FILLED
WITH MAGIC

Posey jumped out of bed and ran
to the window.

It was snowing.

"It's a white Christmas!" Posey cried. "Everyone, get up!"

She ran into the hall. "Mom! Gramps! Wake up!"

Gramps had stayed in the guest room on Christmas Eve. His door was closed. So was her mom's.

Posey ran into Danny's room. Danny stood up in his crib when he saw her.

"It's Christmas, Danny," she said. "It's snowing."

Danny wiggled back and forth like he was dancing.

"Who's making all that ruckus?" Gramps called.

Posey ran back into the hall. "It's snowing, Gramps!"

"Then I guess we all better go back to bed and stay warm," he said.

"Gramps!" Posey protested.

"Don't tease her, Dad." Posey's mom came out of her room. "Merry Christmas, Posey."

Her mom went to change Danny. Gramps started down the stairs.

"Hurry," Posey cried. "Go faster!"

It was a family rule. Everyone had to wait at the top of the stairs until Gramps said they could come down.

It was such a hard rule to follow.

Posey jiggled and hopped. She couldn't stay still. One minute felt like a whole hour.

"Did he come?" Posey called.

There was the thump of the fireplace screen. Posey's mom bounced Danny up and down.

"What's Gramps doing, Mom?" Posey asked.

"Wait just a minute," her mom said. "He is making sure everything's ready."

Christmas music came on. Then twinkly colors glowed in the doorway. Finally, *finally*, Gramps came out into the hall.

"Did he come?" Posey cried.

"Why don't you come and see for yourself?" said Gramps.

Posey ran down the stairs, across the hall, and into the living room.

Santa had come!

The tree sparkled. The snow fell past the windows. The floor was covered with presents.

And here came Mrs. Romero, in through the front door, with snowflakes in her hair.

"Merry Christmas!" everyone called.

Posey's world was filled with magic.

Watch for the next **PRINCESS POSEY** book!

PRINCESS POSEY
and the
FIRST GRADE BOYS

Boys can be so annoying! They make rude noises in class and run around the playground like maniacs. Is it even possible for boys and girls to be friends in first grade?